Sweet Dreams, My Little One

A Treasury of Stories for Bedtime

Snuggle Up, Sleepy Ones

Claire Freedman   Tina Macnaughton

The sun paints the sky
a warm, glowing red.
It's time to stop playing,
it's time for bed.

In the soft swampy mud,
baby hippo, so snug,
Cuddles up close
for a big hippo hug.

Through wild, waving grasses
shy antelope roam.

It's been a long day,
they're ready for home.

Bold leopard cubs rest
from practicing roars.
They snuggle together,
all tired, tangled paws.

While up in the treetops
birds twitter and cheep,

Until quieter and quieter,
they fall fast asleep.

Below in their nests
baby porcupines all
Curl up, snug and tight,
in one spiky ball.

With tired, drooping necks
giraffes flop to the ground.
Sheltered and watched over,
safe and sound.

And mischievous monkeys
shout down from the trees,
"It's not really dark yet.
Five more minutes, please!"

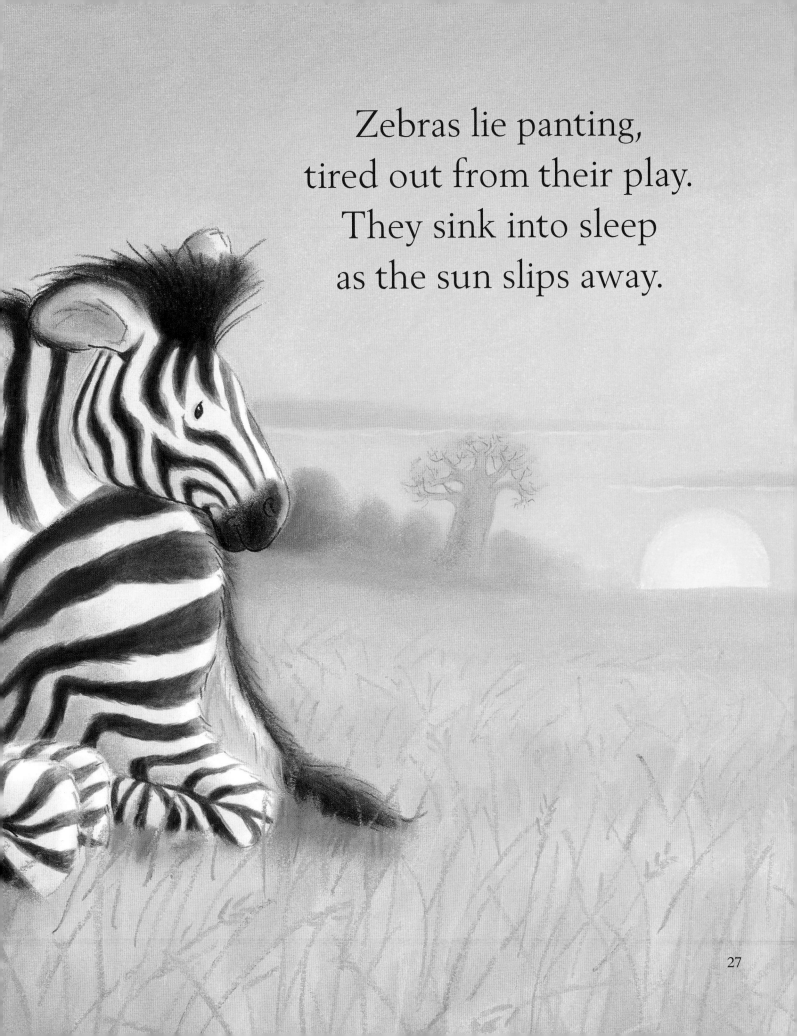

Zebras lie panting,
tired out from their play.
They sink into sleep
as the sun slips away.

Moths go by fluttering,
bats flitter by.
Elephants rumble
their deep lullaby.

Shadows grow deeper,
the lion cubs doze.
Drowsy heads nod,
little eyes start to close.

Stars twinkle brightly,
the moon softly gleams.
Snuggle up, sleepy ones.
Hush now, sweet dreams!

Can't you sleep, Dotty?

★ ★ ★

Tim Warnes

Tick-Tock!
Tick-Tock!

38

Dotty couldn't sleep.
It was her first night
in her new home.

She tried sleeping
upside down.

She tried
snuggling up
to Penguin.

She even tried
lying on the
floor.

AWOOOOOOOOOOOoo

But still Dotty
couldn't sleep.

Dotty's howling woke up Pip the
Mouse. "Can't you sleep, Dotty?"
he asked. "Perhaps you should try
counting the stars like I do."

But Dotty could only count up to one. *That* wasn't enough to send her to sleep.

What could she do next?

AWOOOOOOOOOOOOO

Susie the Bird was awake now. "Can't you sleep, Dotty?" she chirped. "I always have a little drink before I go to bed."

Chirp!
Chirp!

Dotty went to her bowl and
had a little drink.

Slurp!
Slurp!

But then she made
a tiny puddle.
Well *that*
wouldn't help!
What *could* Dotty
do to get to sleep?

AWOOOOOOOOOoo..

Whiskers the Rabbit had woken up, too.
"Can't you sleep, Dotty?" he mumbled
sleepily. "I hide in my den at bedtime.
That always works."

Dotty dived under her blanket so that only her bottom was showing. But it was very dark under there with no light at all.

Dotty was too scared to go to sleep.

AWOOOOOOOOOOoooo

Flump!

Tommy the Tortoise poked his head from out of his shell.

"Can't you sleep, Dotty?" he sighed. "I like to sleep where it's bright and sunny."

Plod
Plod

Dotty liked the idea . . .

and turned on her flashlight!

"Turn it off, Dotty!"
shouted all her friends.
"*We* can't get to sleep now!"

Poor Dotty was too
tired to try anything else.
Then Tommy had a great idea!

He helped Dotty into her bed.
What Dotty needed for the first
night in her new home was . . .

to snuggle among *all*
her new friends. Soon
they were all fast asleep.
Good night, Dotty.

Little Bunny's Bathtime!

Jane Johnson

pictures by

Gaby Hansen

"Bathtime for my little rabbits!"
called Mrs. Rabbit, and her
children came running.
All except her youngest
little one.

"I don't want a bath,"
said Little Bunny.
"I want to keep playing."

67

"You really want to play all by
yourself?" asked Mrs. Rabbit.
Little Bunny nodded, but
now he wasn't so sure.

"Well, you be good while
I'm busy with the others,"
said Mrs. Rabbit, plopping
her bunnies into the bathtub.

"Swish, splish, splash,"
   sang the little rabbits happily,
   swirling their bubbles around.
      Little Bunny wanted
   to play, too.

"Look at me!" he called,
hiding behind the towels.

"Yes, dear," said Mrs. Rabbit, but
she went on washing the others.
"Tickly, wiggly, giggly toes," sang
the little rabbits as they wiggled their
feet in the water.

"Guess where I am?"
shouted Little Bunny,
hidden in the
laundry basket.

"Found you," smiled his
mother, lifting the lid.

But she turned back
to finish washing
the others.

"Out you go," puffed Mrs. Rabbit,
lifting her children out of the tub.

"Rub-a-dub-dub, you've all had a scrub,"
she laughed. "What lovely, clean
bunnies you are!"

Little Bunny was upset.
He wanted his mommy
to notice him.

So he
climbed
up . . .

and up . . .

as far as he could.

But suddenly . . .

SPLASH!

He fell into the bathtub!

"Oh my!" cried Mrs. Rabbit, scooping
him out of the water right away.
Little Bunny gazed up at her happily.
"I'm ready for my bath now, Mommy,"
he said, smiling sweetly.

Mrs. Rabbit couldn't
help smiling back.
"Off you go to play
quietly," she said to
her other rabbits.

Then she ran
fresh water and gave
Little Bunny his
own special bath.

"Soapy ears and soapy toes, and soapy little
bunny nose!" sang Mrs. Rabbit.
She washed his ears while he played
with the new bubbles.
"I love you, Mommy," said Little Bunny.
"I love you too, sweetheart!"

She washed his back while
he played with his boat.
  "You're the best mommy in the
whole world," said Little Bunny.
  "And you're my precious
little bunnykin."

She dried his fur
and whiskers, and said,
"Mmm, you smell
so nice and clean!"

And Little Bunny kissed his mommy
and hugged her tight.

"There now, all done," sighed Mrs. Rabbit.
"It's time for bed. Where are my other
little rabbits?"

She found them in the kitchen.
"Oh no! What a mess!" cried
Mrs. Rabbit. "You're all dirty again.
You all need another bath!"

"Yes," giggled Little Bunny.
"All except me!"

Deep, deep in the jungle, chimps were chattering,
frogs were croaking,

birds were chirping, and a million insects
were humming and buzzing. That's a lot of noise!

It was time for Baby Leo to take his morning nap.
"He'll never get to sleep with all this noise," said Mama Lion
to Leo's father. "Isn't there something you can do?"

"Do?" said Papa Lion. "Do? I am king of all the animals. Of course there is something I can do!" He stood up tall, puffed out his huge chest, and roared . . .

And so, Baby Leo fell asleep. Then Papa Lion whispered
softly, but clearly so that all the creatures could hear him:
"If any of you makes a noise, and wakes up Leo, I will gobble you up."

And all was quiet in the jungle.
Quiet as the morning mist. Quiet as the opening flowers.
Quiet as a baby sleeping. Suddenly . . .

Cawing and crowing, squeaking and squawking.
Beaks pecking and claws scratching.
Two parrots were arguing
in the bushes!

"Quiet!" said Papa Lion, as loud as he dared,
in case Baby Leo was still sleeping.
"It's all right," said Mama Lion. "Leo's fast asleep."
"Oh, well," said Papa Lion. "But I could have used a snack."

Once again, all was quiet in the jungle.
Quiet as the trees growing toward the sky.
Quiet as the leaves reaching toward the light.
Quiet as a baby sleeping. Suddenly . . .

Chuckling
and chortling,

sniggering
and snickering.

The hyena was laughing.
Laughing like hyenas do.

But nobody knew what was so funny.

"Quiet!" said Papa Lion, as loud as he dared,
in case his son was still sleeping.
"It's all right," said Mama Lion. "He's still asleep."
"Oh, well," said Papa Lion. "But I am getting hungry."

Then all was quiet in the jungle.
Quiet as the calm after a storm.
Quiet as sunshine after rain.
Quiet as a baby sleeping. Suddenly . . .

Howling and hooting, screeching and chattering.
Swinging and swooping. A family of monkeys was
leaping through the trees!

"Quiet!" said Papa Lion, as loud as he dared,
just in case Leo was still sleeping.
"It's all right," said Mama Lion. "Leo's asleep."
"Oh, well," said Papa Lion. "But now I'm very hungry."

It was the middle of the day
and the jungle was hot and humid.
The animals crept into the shade of the
trees, drowsy and dozing.

And all was quiet in the jungle.
Quiet as the blazing sun.
Quiet as the shadows underneath the trees.
Quiet as a baby sleeping. Suddenly . . .

Splashing and squelching.

Oohing and aahing.

A hippopotamus was
yawning in the cool, muddy
shallows of the river.

"Quiet!" said Papa Lion, as loud as he dared,
in case the baby lion was still sleeping.
"It's all right," said Mama Lion. "Leo's fast asleep."
"Humph!" said Papa Lion. "I guess my eyes are bigger
than my belly."

But Papa Lion rubbed his tummy and began to think,
"I do wish someone would make just a
little more noise and wake up Baby Leo.
Just for a minute."

Yet all remained quiet in the jungle.
Quiet as a fish swimming in the river.
Quiet as a bird soaring in the sky.
Quiet as a baby sleeping. Suddenly . . .

113

A rumbling and growling,
a groaning and moaning,

a gurgling
and burbling.

A noise like nothing ever heard before!
Loud as thunder. Loud as a banging drum.
Loud as a baby crying!

"Who has woken up Baby Leo?"
cried Mama Lion.
"Find who it was, Papa! Now!"

"It's me," said Papa Lion, meekly.
"My stomach is rumbling.
Because I'm so hungry!"

Time to Sleep, Alfie Bear!

Catherine Walters

"It's nearly bedtime, Alfie," called
Mother Bear. She gathered up Alfie's baby
brother and sister, but Alfie didn't move.
    "It can't be bedtime," he complained.
"It's still light."
    "It's always light at bedtime in the
summer," said Mother Bear. "Come on,
Alfie, time for your bath."

123

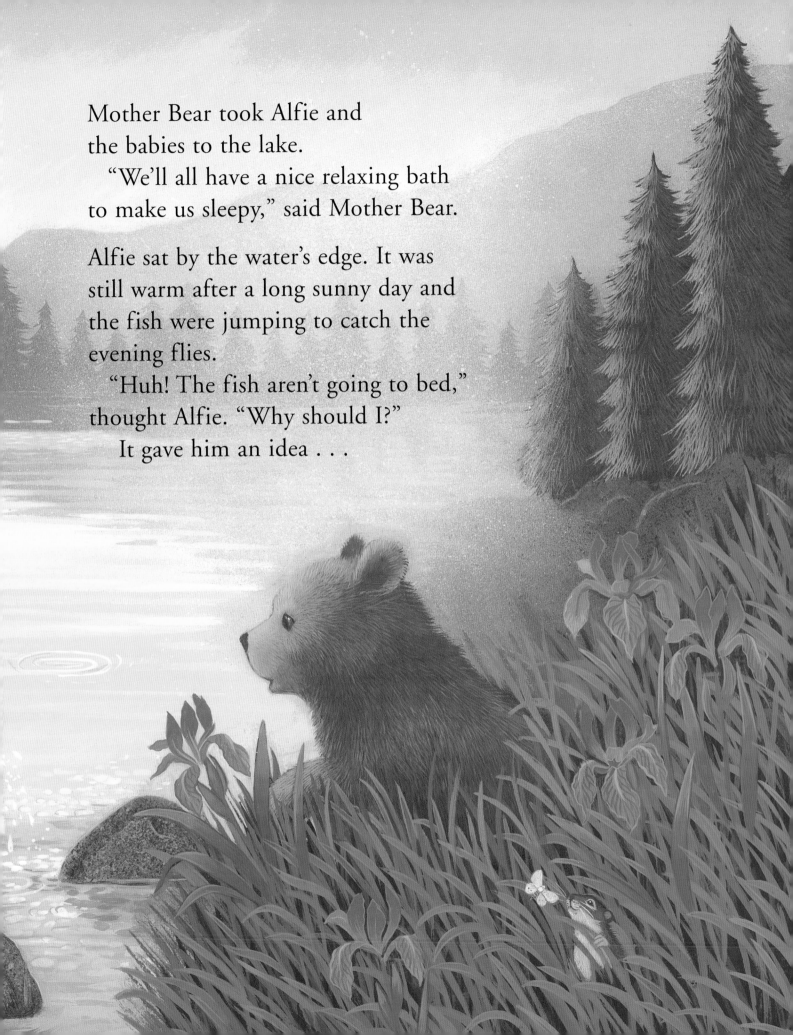

Mother Bear took Alfie and
the babies to the lake.

"We'll all have a nice relaxing bath
to make us sleepy," said Mother Bear.

Alfie sat by the water's edge. It was
still warm after a long sunny day and
the fish were jumping to catch the
evening flies.

"Huh! The fish aren't going to bed,"
thought Alfie. "Why should I?"

It gave him an idea . . .

"Look, Mother Bear," shouted Alfie.
"I don't have to go to bed! I'm a fish!"

He began to jump and dive and splash.
The babies loved it. They laughed and
splashed too.

"Don't do that," sighed Mother Bear.
"The babies are getting too excited.
They'll never go to sleep."

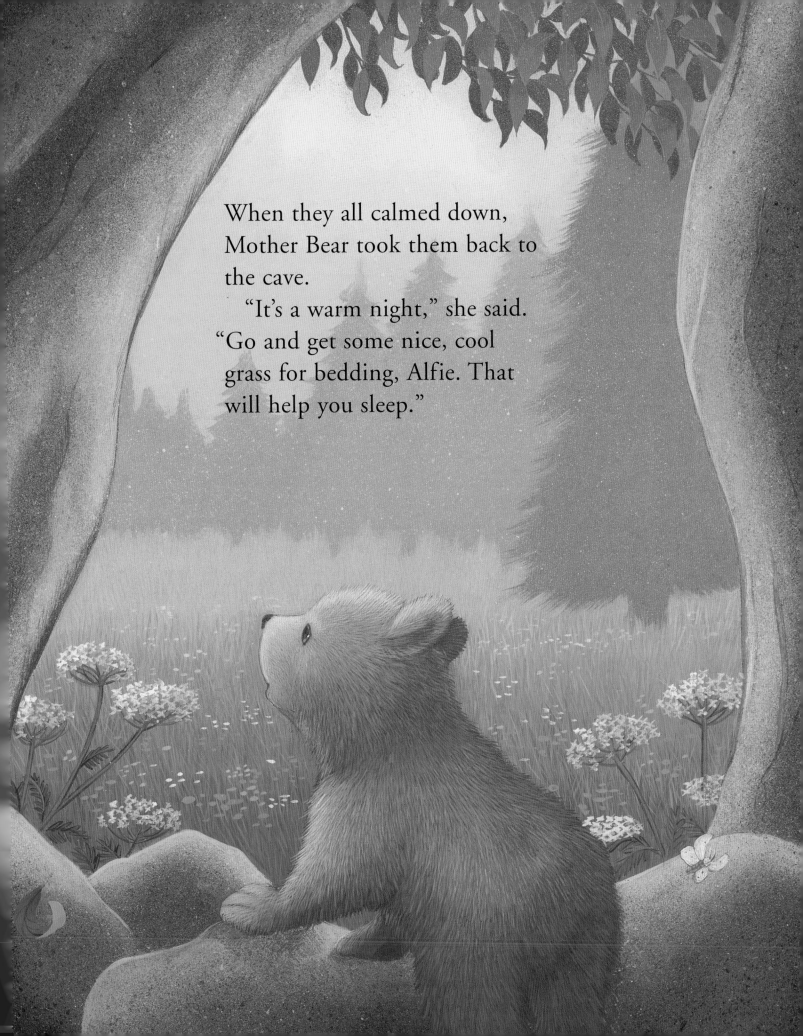

When they all calmed down, Mother Bear took them back to the cave.

"It's a warm night," she said. "Go and get some nice, cool grass for bedding, Alfie. That will help you sleep."

Alfie went outside and pulled
up a few pawfuls of grass.

Over in the meadow, some owls were
swooping, ready for their evening hunt.
"The owls aren't going to bed,"
thought Alfie. "Why should I?"

Alfie rushed back into the cave and began
to flap his arms. Grass flew everywhere.

"Look! I'm an owl!" he hooted. "I don't
need to go to bed. I'm just getting up!"

"Oh Alfie, stop that!" groaned Mother
Bear. "Look, the babies are throwing all
their lovely bedding around, too. None
of you will have anywhere to sleep."

At last, Alfie and the babies were safely
in bed but still they didn't go to sleep.

"I think you need a nice, gentle song,"
said Mother Bear. "Now, close your eyes."

Alfie wasn't listening. Outside, he
could hear wolves howling.

"The wolves aren't going to sleep,"
he thought. "Why should I?"

"Look, I'm a wolf! HOOOOWL!" said Alfie.

"OW, OW, OW!" shrieked the babies, kicking their feet.

Mother Bear wasn't pleased. "That's enough, Alfie," she growled. "I don't want any little wolves in the cave. You can wait outside until the babies are asleep."

"Hooray!" cried Alfie, running outside.
The sun had set and the air was full
of dust and shadows. Alfie charged
across the meadow, tipped back his
head, and howled again,
"HOOOOWL!"
Then, from somewhere close by,
someone answered him,
"HOOOOWL!"

Alfie jumped. There in front of him was
a wolf cub, with his family close by.

The cub sniffed him all over.

"Are you a wolf?" it asked. "You sound
like one, but you don't look like one."

"All little wolf cubs should be in bed
by now," growled Mother Wolf.

"Are you sure you're a wolf?" called
a big, gruff voice . . .

". . . because you look like a little bear to me!"
     It was Father Bear, coming to take
him home.
     "I'm a bear, I'm a bear!" shouted Alfie.
     The big wolves turned and walked away.
     "Goodnight, little bear," called the
wolf cub, following them into the trees.

Father Bear snuggled Alfie into his fur.

"So you're a bear?" he said. "But are you a sleepy bear all ready for bed?"

Night had fallen, and the sky sparkled with stars.

"No," said Alfie. "I'm not–"

But before he could finish speaking, he had fallen fast asleep.

Two Hungry Bears

Linda Cornwell and Jane Chapman

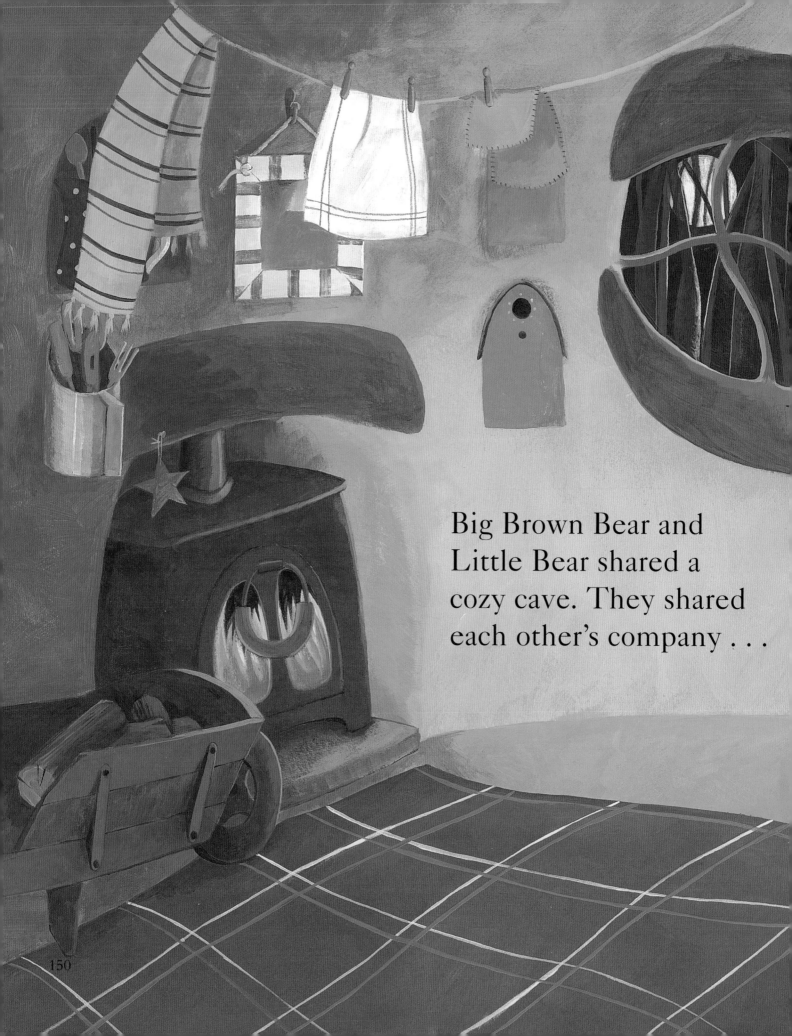

Big Brown Bear and
Little Bear shared a
cozy cave. They shared
each other's company . . .

150

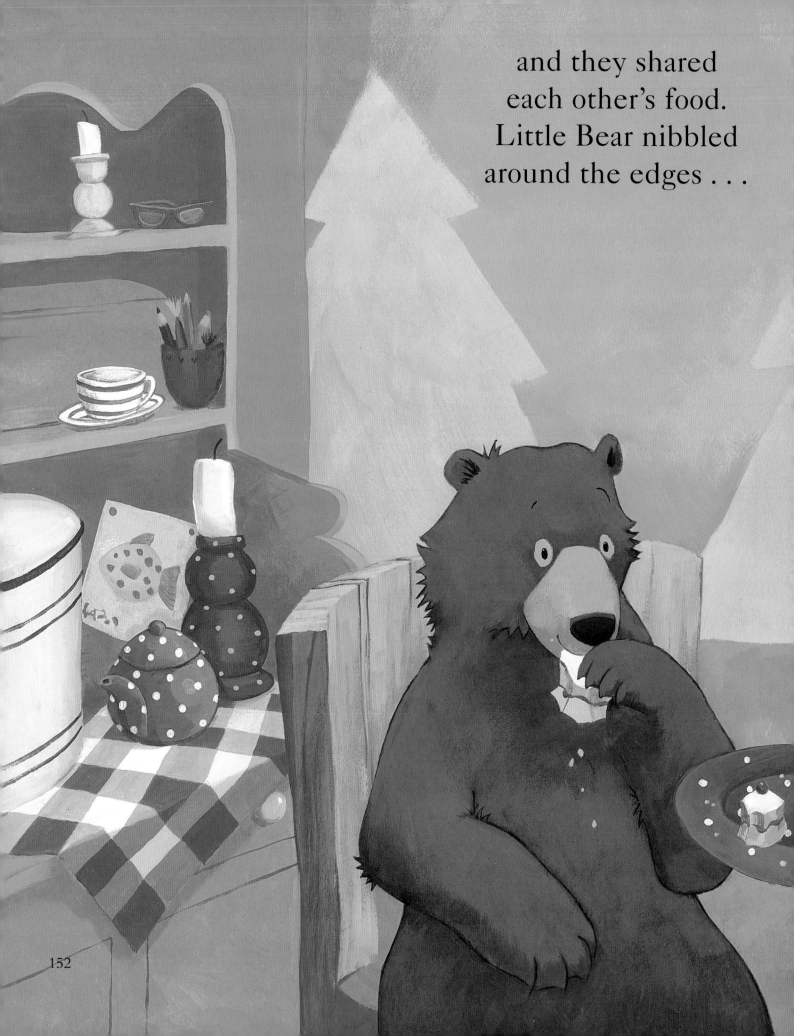

and they shared
each other's food.
Little Bear nibbled
around the edges . . .

152

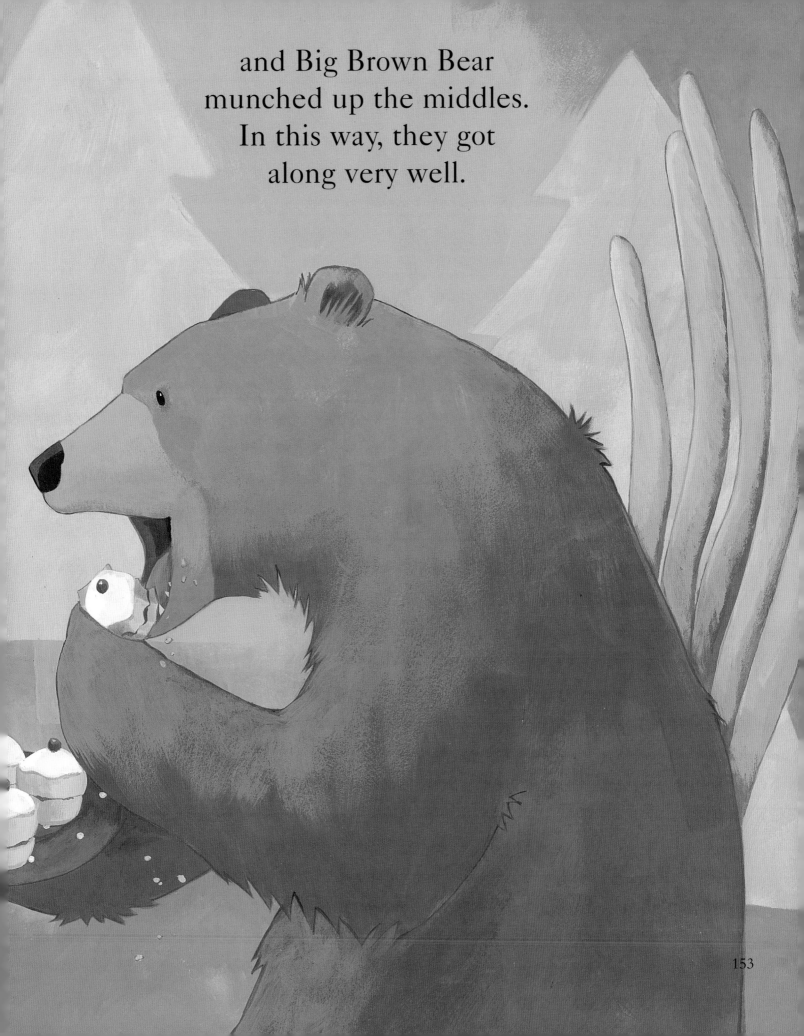

and Big Brown Bear
munched up the middles.
In this way, they got
along very well.

But one bright autumn day, Little Bear woke up feeling EXTRA hungry and Big Brown Bear woke up feeling MONSTROUSLY hungry!

"I'll buy some food for both of us," said Little Bear.

"That's very kind of you, Little Bear," answered Big Brown Bear sleepily, and he crept right back to bed.

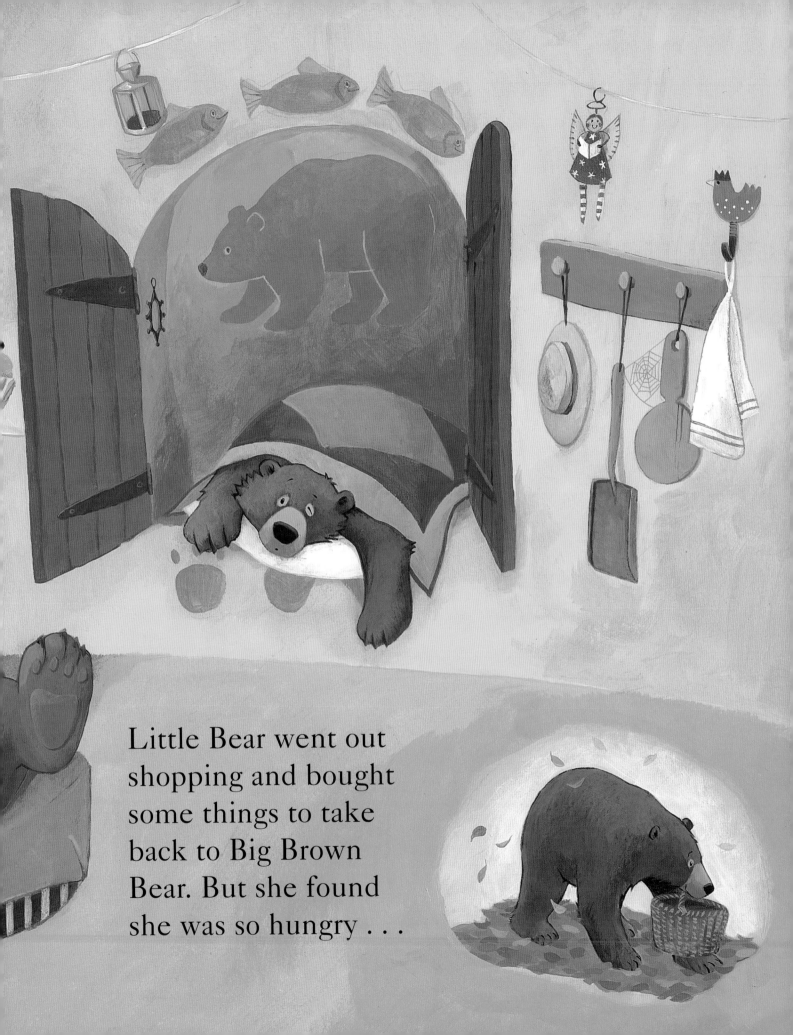

Little Bear went out shopping and bought some things to take back to Big Brown Bear. But she found she was so hungry . . .

that she ate everything
straight away—
pies and pastries,
peanuts and puddings,

chocolates and cheeses,
crisps and cakes—

from sides to middles,
middles to sides
AND BACK AGAIN!

Meanwhile, Big Brown Bear's tummy was
RRRRUMMMBLING very loudly—so loudly
that the walls of the cave began to shake.
"I've been thinking," said Big Brown Bear,
"maybe *I* should be out shopping for Little Bear."
So off he went with his big bag . . .

but when he had filled
it right up, he found
he was so hungry,
he could not wait.

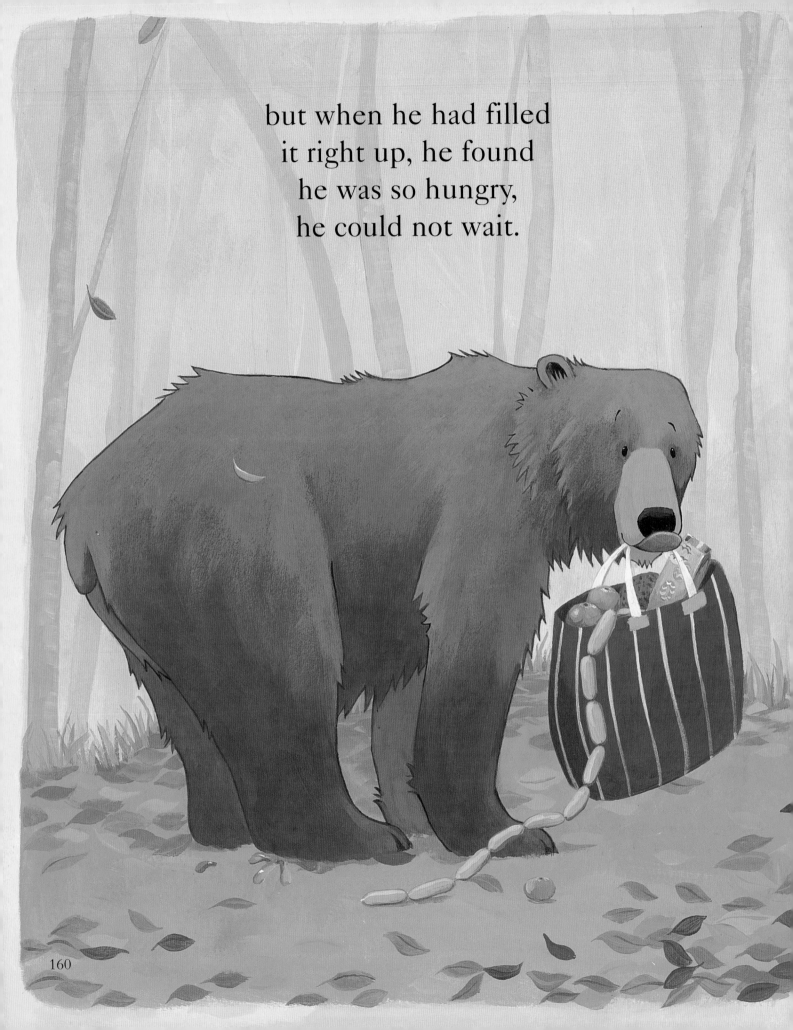

He began by
munching just
the middles.

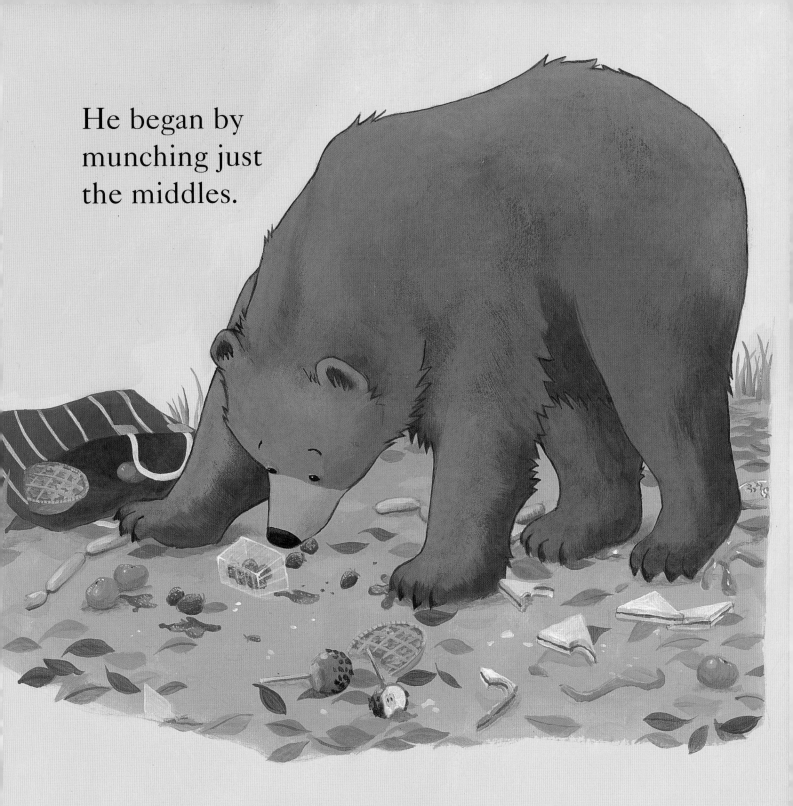

But then he set to work on sausages,
strawberries and sandwiches,
not to mention tangerines,
caramel apples and peach pies . . .

AND
hamburgers,
custard and
fries . . .

AND
biscuits,
spaghetti
and soup . . .

AND
pizzas, salads and
ice-cream . . .

AND
tomatoes,
jello and
corn on the cob—
and one small
grape.

163

Big Brown Bear ate tops, bottoms,
sides, and middles.
There was just no stopping him!

But when he had finished eating,
he began to feel very, very full
and very, very guilty.
He had nothing left for Little Bear.

Big Brown Bear staggered back home where
Little Bear was waiting patiently for him.
"Did you find any nice middles to munch?"
Little Bear asked him. *I can see that you did!*
she thought to herself.
Big Brown Bear could only nod his head.

"Did you come across any tasty edges to nibble?"
asked Big Brown Bear. *It certainly looks as
though you might have!* he thought to himself.

They sat
down together—
very carefully.
"I saved you half
of a cracker,"
said Big Brown Bear.
"It still has four
edges to nibble."
"I saved you three
quarters of a banana,"
said Little Bear.
"It's all middle—
no edges
at all!"

169

After a while, Big
Brown Bear yawned.
"I think I'll skip supper,"
he said. "I'm feeling
a little too tired."
"An early night will
do us both good,"
agreed Little Bear.
They spent an awfully
long time brushing
their teeth . . .

before Big Brown Bear snuggled into his
bed, and Little Bear crept quietly into hers.
"Let's buy the food together tomorrow,"
said Big Brown Bear with a yawn.
But tomorrow was a long, long time away
because . . .

Big Brown Bear and
Little Bear slept, with
their tummies pleasantly full,
all through the winter until
SPRING!